To my dear mother,
who understood about birthdays

—LJ

Happy Birthday

—PM

Text copyright © 1999 by Lynne Jonell.
Illustrations copyright © 1999 by Petra Mathers. All rights reserved.
This book, or parts thereof, may not be reproduced in any form without
permission in writing from the publisher. G. P. Putnam's Sons, a division of
Penguin Putnam Books for Young Readers, 345 Hudson Street, New York, NY 10014.
G. P. Putnam's Sons, Reg. U.S. Pat. & Tm. Off. Published simultaneously in Canada.
Printed in Hong Kong by South China Printing Co. (1988) Ltd.
Book designed by Cecilia Yung and Donna Mark. Text set in Catchup.
Library of Congress Cataloging-in-Publication Data
Jonell, Lynne. It's my birthday, too! / written by Lynne Jonell;
illustrated by Petra Mathers. p. cm. Summary: Christopher would rather have
a dog than a little brother who ruins his birthday parties, but when his brother
begins to act like a puppy Christopher has a change of heart. [1. Brothers—Fiction.
2. Parties—Fiction. 3. Birthdays—Fiction. 4. Dogs—Fiction.] I. Mathers, Petra, ill.
II. Title. PZ7.J675It 1999 [E]—dc21 97-49635 CIP AC
ISBN 0-399-23323-7
3 5 7 9 10 8 6 4

IT'S MY BIRTHDAY, TOO!

WRITTEN BY Lynne Jonell

ILLUSTRATED BY Petra Mathers

G. P. PUTNAM'S SONS   NEW YORK

Mommy frosted a cake.

Daddy blew up balloons.

Christopher said, "Happy Birthday to ME!"

"It's my birthday, too," said Robbie.

"It is NOT your birthday," said Christopher.
"It is mine, and I am going to have a party."
"I get to come, too," said Robbie.

"You came last year," said Christopher,
"and you wrecked everything."
"I'm bigger now," said Robbie.
"You are not big enough," said Christopher.

"You will not know how to play the games.
You will sing the wrong words to
'Happy Birthday.'
And you will try to open all my presents."

"I will only open my own presents," said Robbie.
"You don't get any," said Christopher.
"You are not the birthday boy.
You are just the brother."

Robbie was mad.

"You are being mean on purpose," he said.

"If I can't come to your party,

then I won't **be** your brother."

"Good," said Christopher.
"I don't want a brother, anyway.
I'd rather have a puppy."
Robbie looked up. "Would you let
a puppy come to your party?"

"Well . . . maybe," said Christopher.
"If he was a very **good** puppy.
He couldn't bite. And he would have to
obey all my commands. . . ."

"I guess you **are** well trained," said Christopher,
and he scratched Robbie behind the ears.

The doorbell rang.
"Down, boy," said Christopher.
"How do you like my new puppy?"
he said to his friends.

"He's kind of scruffy-looking," said Andy.

"Eeew!" said Kyle. "Doggie breath!"

Lindsay patted his head. "Can he do tricks?"

"Sure," said Christopher.

"See?" said Christopher. "He's smart."
"Wow," said the kids.

At the party, the puppy tried hard to behave.
He did not know how to play the games.
So he chewed a shoelace instead.
"Did you have to drool on it?" said Christopher.

The puppy could not sing "Happy Birthday."

But he knew how to howl along.

The puppy did not get to open any presents.
But he had a very good time
playing with the wrappings.
"I should have put you on a leash," said
Christopher, and he threw the wrappings away.

Robbie fetched them.
"You dumb puppy," said Christopher.
"If I give you a doggy treat,
will you stay out of trouble?"

"Woof!" said Robbie,
and he leapt onto the table.
"He's a bad dog," said Andy.
"You should swat him with a newspaper."

Robbie whimpered.

"He's not **that** bad," said Christopher.

"He's kind of messy, though," said Kyle.

"Look at the chocolate on his nose!"

"It will wipe off," said Christopher.

Robbie wagged his tail. Then he gave a little yip.
"He says he likes you best," said Lindsay.

"You're lucky," said Kyle.
"I wish I had a puppy," said Andy.

"HA!" said Christopher.
"Puppies are nothing but trouble.
"*I'd* rather have a brother."